This Book
Belongs To:

....

....

Animal Stories

Animal Stories

Bath • New York • Singapore • Hong Kong • Cologne • Delhi
Melbourne • Amsterdam • Johannesburg • Auckland • Shenzhen

Illustrated by Claire Henley

This edition published by Parragon in 2011

Parragon
Queen Street House
4 Queen Street
Bath BA1 1HE, UK

Copyright © Parragon Books Ltd 2003

ISBN 978-1-4454-1980-0

Printed in China

Contents

Dance Jiggle, Dance!

All the animals at Windy Farm are getting a bit fed up. They can hear Jiggle the donkey from inside the barn. He has put music on and he is tap-dancing.

Jiggle loves to dance. He has read in the local paper about a dancing competition, and he is determined to win. But first he has to find a partner.

Jiggle goes over to the pond to ask Duck. "I'd like to help," says Duck, "but I've got flat feet."

Next, Jiggle goes to the sty to ask Pig, but he's too muddy to dance.

Then Jiggle goes to the barn to ask Cow.

"I can't," says Cow. "My milk will get too frothy. Go and ask Sheep."

"Sheep," asks Jiggle, "will you dance with me in the competition next week?"

"It's much too hot to dance, Jiggle," replies Sheep, fanning herself with a large leaf. "I've got such a thick coat, I shall melt if I move quickly. Ask Hen – she can't keep still for two minutes."

Hen's too busy laying eggs to dance though.

But Jiggle refuses to be put off. He practises tap-dancing in the barn every day. All the animals are getting more and more fed up with the sound of his tapping feet.

The day of the competition arrives. It is warm and sunny and the village green looks very festive. There are tents and stalls and games and lots of delicious things to eat.

From the biggest tent comes the sound of music. Jiggle goes into the tent to watch. First, two pigs dance a waltz. Then, two chickens dance a tango and two cows

do a break-dance. They are all very good, especially the cows.

Soon it's the turn of Farmer Brown and Mrs Brown. All the animals cheer loudly and stamp their hooves. But, as they make their way to the stage, Farmer Brown trips over Constance the cat. He falls heavily and bangs his knee. The music starts. But Farmer Brown can't get up.

Mrs Brown looks round and sees Jiggle. "Will you be my partner?" she asks.

Will he? Jiggle can't wait to start dancing!

The pair dance superbly. Jiggle has never danced so well, he moves like lightning across the stage and Mrs Brown keeps up with him. Their feet tap together in perfect rhythm.

The judge has no doubts about which pair should receive the first prize. It is the happiest day of Jiggle's life.

Now the other animals don't mind Jiggle's dancing quite so much. Mrs Brown has given him some new music, and on one of them there is singing. Sometimes, Jiggle even joins in!

Whenever he does, the other animals cover up their ears and groan,

"Oh, no, Jiggle!"

Blossom the Cow

At the top of the hill was a farm. Farmer Pinstripe looked after Blossom the cow and the other animals. Mrs Pinstripe looked after the visitors who came to stay on the farm on holiday.

One Monday morning at breakfast, Mrs Pinstripe noticed that none of her visitors had eaten their breakfast, because the milk tasted funny.

"I can't understand it," she said. "Yesterday's milk was lovely."

That night she complained to Farmer Pinstripe, "It must be that cow of yours, Blossom." Farmer Pinstripe scratched his head. He couldn't understand it either. Blossom's milk was the best he'd ever tasted. She had won prizes for it. What could be wrong? He would have to keep an eye on her.

Farmer Pinstripe decided to watch Blossom wherever she went.

All that day, he watched Blossom eat grass and her milk tasted lovely!

For the next few days, Farmer Pinstripe followed Blossom everywhere. He still found nothing wrong.

On Sunday, Blossom seemed excited. She almost skipped as Farmer Pinstripe let her into the field. Then, instead of going to the top field or middle field, she went straight down to the pretty stream at the bottom of the hill, and waited.

Soon, a group of children came into the field with a big blue picnic box.

Blossom stood close to the children, as if she was one of the gang. They made a big fuss of her, scratching her behind her ears and blowing gently on her face.

Then they opened the picnic box and Blossom saw what she had been waiting for...

It was the salt and vinegar crisps!

Blossom gobbled them up... and the cheese and onion crisps, and the spicy barbecue flavoured ones too. She liked everything with a strong taste!

Farmer Pinstripe was amazed.

"So," he said to himself, "that's why the milk tastes so funny on Monday mornings."

That evening Farmer Pinstripe gave Blossom a handful of extra-strong peppermints. She loved them so much he let her eat the whole packet. Then he waited a while before he milked her.

On Monday morning, while the guests were eating their breakfast, Mrs Pinstripe watched carefully.

The visitors ate everything!

Mrs Pinstripe was very relieved.

After the last visitor had left to go home, Mr and Mrs Pinstripe read their comments in the visitors' book they kept in the hall.

They had written: "We had a lovely holiday. We loved the farm and all the animals. Mrs Pinstripe looked after us very well. The food was wonderful, and especially… the peppermint-flavoured yoghurt!"

I'll Have to Think Again

A frog sat on a large lily-pad, reading a cookery book.

"Flour, milk, eggs and honey," he muttered. "That shouldn't be difficult." It was Frog's birthday and he wanted to make a huge birthday cake and invite all his friends to tea. He'd never made a cake before, but he was sure it would be easy.

Of course, he needed the ingredients first.

"Flour," he gulped, as he plopped into the river and swam to the mill.

When Frog explained what he wanted to the miller, he smiled.

"No problem," grinned the miller. "But how will you get the flour home?"

"Oh!" said Frog, surprised. He hadn't thought about that. "I'll have to think again!"

Frog leapt back into the cool river and swam towards the meadow.

"I'll get the milk first. Brown Cow won't mind giving me some milk," Frog thought.

"Of course you can have some milk," Brown Cow told Frog, "but what will you carry it in?"

"Oh!" said Frog, surprised. He hadn't thought about that. "I'll have to think again!"

Frog slid down the river bank and set off upstream.

"Perhaps I should get the eggs first," Frog gurgled to himself, hopping up to the hen house.

"Take as many as you need," Speckled Hen told Frog, "but how will you get the eggs home? You have no basket."

"Oh!" said Frog, surprised. He hadn't thought about that. "I'll have to think again."

Frog hopped across the farmyard, past the farmhouse and through the hedge.

"I am silly!" croaked Frog. "I should have got the honey first." He jumped down the lane to the beekeeper's cottage.

The beekeeper was happy to give Frog some honey.

"I don't think I should give you a jar, though," he said. "If it drops and breaks you're sure to cut yourself, but..."

Frog didn't wait for him to finish.

"It's all right," he croaked huskily, as a tear fell from the corner of his eye. "I'll just have to think again." And he limped off down the lane.

By the time he got back to the lily-pad he had no idea how he could get the ingredients for his birthday cake.

Suddenly Frog heard singing:

"Happy Birthday to you, Happy Birthday to you...!"

On the bank of the pond stood all his friends. And the miller was holding a huge birthday cake.

"How very kind," said Frog quietly. "But I was going to make a cake to surprise you."

"Well," laughed his friends together, "you'll have to think again."

Elephants Don't Eat Jelly

Jessica was really looking forward to going to the zoo with her family. She loved animals and she wanted to see as many as possible. The lions, the elephants, the monkeys, the penguins, the giraffes... oh, and the ant eaters!

She didn't tell anyone, but she had planned to give each animal a special treat.

When they got to the zoo, their first stop was the elephants. Jessica looked at their huge feet, their legs like tree trunks, and their big heads with very small eyes. Jessica watched as an elephant picked a nut from the ground with the tip of his trunk and put it in his mouth.

She took her bag off her back and opened it. Then she took out a little pot of red jelly and a white plastic spoon.

"Do elephants eat jelly?" she asked.

"No, elephants don't eat jelly," laughed Mum.

"And look," pointed Dad, "there's a notice which says PLEASE DON'T FEED THE ELEPHANTS."

Jessica put the pot of jelly back into her bag. As they moved away, the elephant began to bellow loudly.

"I think he really did want the jelly!" she said.

They could still hear the noise when they reached the monkeys, climbing trees, hanging upside down, and pulling rude faces.

Jessica opened her bag and took out a small packet.

"Do monkeys eat chocolate biscuits?" she asked, as a monkey came close.

"No, monkeys don't eat chocolate biscuits," said Dad. And he pointed to a notice which said PLEASE DON'T FEED THE MONKEYS.

"I think he really did want the chocolate biscuits," said Jessica as they moved away.

They came to the penguins, waddling along. A man appeared with a bucket of fish. He threw the fish in the pool and the penguins dived in. When they were swimming they looked quite different. They were fast and energetic.

"Do penguins eat cheese triangles?" Jessica inquired, holding a box in her hands up to the man.

"No," said the man, smiling. "Penguins don't eat cheese triangles."

When he moved out of the way Jessica could see the notice which said PLEASE DON'T FEED

PLEASE
DON'T FEED
THE
PENGUINS

THE PENGUINS.

It was the same with the giraffes. They didn't eat barbeque flavoured crisps!

The lions didn't eat yoghurts!

The parrots didn't eat dolly mixtures!

And the ant eaters only ate ants!

"Never mind," said Mum, "we are going to have a picnic now. You can get out all the special treats and feed your baby brother instead!"

So that's what Jessica did.

It was nearly as much fun as feeding the animals!

No Time!

Autumn had come, and Scurry the squirrel was in a hurry collecting nuts for winter. He had no time for anything else. He didn't even have time to see his friends.

"Hello, Scurry," called Milly Mouse, halfway through the morning. "Would you like to come and see my winter bed."

"No time!" muttered Scurry. "I'm in a hurry."

At lunchtime, Walter Woodpecker swooped down onto a branch of Scurry's tree.

"Do you want to come and see the great hole I've pecked in a tree?" he asked.

"No time!" snapped Scurry. "I'm in a hurry."

Halfway through the afternoon, Rocky Rabbit hopped by.

"Scurry, my friend," he smiled. "I've been practising my digging. Why don't you come and watch me dig a burrow?"

"No time!" yelled Scurry. "I'm in a hurry."

All afternoon, Scurry collected nuts. As darkness fell, he scampered up his tree, into the hole near the top of the trunk, and curled up to sleep.

Not long afterwards, a great storm began to howl through the forest. Scurry woke up to find the tree shaking wildly, until...

With a great CRACK! over the tree went, and Scurry with it.

When the wind stopped blowing, Scurry poked his nose out of his ruined home. What was he going to do?

"Help!" he called.

Milly appeared.

"Don't worry, Scurry," said Milly. "Come and share my warm bed. We'll sort things out in the morning."

"My lovely tree," sobbed Scurry the next morning. "Where will I find a comfortable hole like that again?"

"Easy!" said a voice. It was Walter. "Come and see the great hole I made."

"You're right," said Scurry when he had tried the hole. "It's even better than my old home. But how am I going to get all the nuts from my winter store moved? They're buried under the fallen tree."

"No problem," said a voice.

It was Rocky.

"I can dig under
that old tree in

no time, get the nuts out, and carry them to your new home.

When the work was over, Scruffy called his friends together.

"I want you all to come to tea with me," he told them. "It's a thank you for helping me."

"Sorry," said Milly and Walter and Rocky all together. "No time! We're in a hurry."

Scurry hung his head. Then the three friends burst out laughing.

"Oh, Scurry," they said. "We're not in a hurry. For a friend, we've always got time."